The Safari Children's Books
on Good Behavior

Ellena the Elephant Learns Why she Needs to Tidy Up her Toys

by
Cressida Elias

Illustrated by Carriel Ann Santos

ISBN-13: 978-1475101270
ISBN-10: 1475101279

Ellena the Elephant was a very neat girl.

She loved to wear a bow on her head and brush her tail everyday.

Looking good was important to her.

However, the same could not be said for her toys!

She did not tidy them up when she was asked to and they just lay around her room in a mess.

In fact, her toys were not just left untidily in *her* room, but soon they were left all around the rest of the house as well...

in the living room...

in the kitchen...

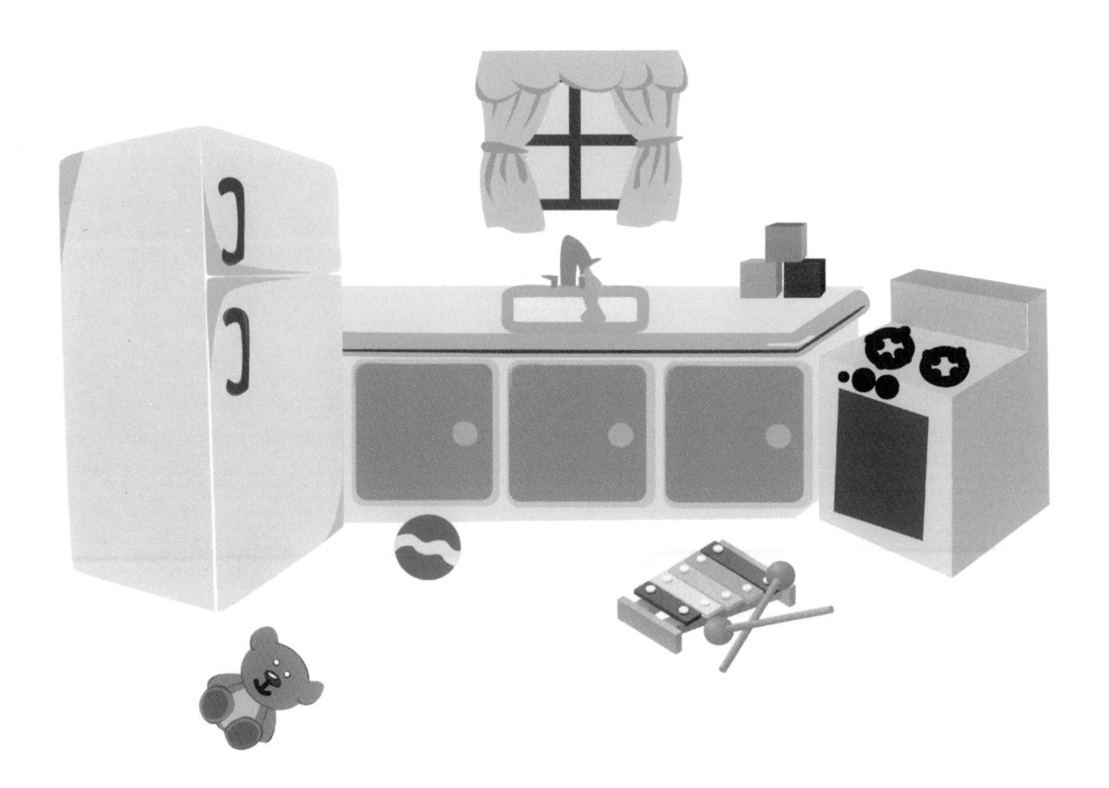

and by the front door!

Now Ellena's parents told her many times to tidy up her toys.

Why?

Because if she left them all over the place, somebody might tread on them. And if one of the other elephants trod on them, well...they would definitely break!

They told her that if she did not have neat and tidy toys, how could she find her favorite one that she wanted to play with?

Now Ellena thought about this and decided that it would be quite sensible to keep her toys tidy, so she could find them easily and keep them in good shape.

So she started to put her toys away.

But after a while, she ran off to play with her friends and forgot about tidying up.

Later on she came home for her dinner.

After eating well, she decided she wanted to play with her favorite toy...a little dog on wheels.

But where was it? She looked in her bedroom and then in the kitchen. Oh dear... there were lots of toys everywhere but the little dog wasn't there.

'Hmm...', she thought, 'Where did I leave it?'

Suddenly she heard a loud cry! She ran to the living room.

It was her brother, Edgar, he had put his foot on something and it had really hurt him.

'Ouch!' he said, 'Ellena, I've trod on your toy dog and it has made my foot really sore!'

'Whoops', thought Ellena. She remembered that she had left it on the floor in the living room. It was *her* fault that Edgar hurt his foot.

'Sorry, Edgar,' she said, then she looked at the toy. It was all broken into tiny pieces next to Edgar.

She started to cry because this was her favorite toy. This made Edgar feel bad.

But then Ellena remembered what her mother and father had told her.

She remembered that her mother had asked her to put her toys away, so that they did not get crushed by the heavy feet of other elephants.

Ellena realised that if she had put her toy dog away somewhere safe it would not be broken and Edgar would not have a sore foot!

'Edgar,' she said, 'I hope your foot gets better quickly.

Don't feel bad about my toy dog - it's broken because I didn't put it away.

I'm going to tidy up my toys now, so this doesn't happen again.'

Ellena's mother and father watched her clear up all her toys.

She put them in her toy box next to her bed.

Her parents were very proud of her. They put their long trunks around her and lifted her up.

'Gosh,' thought Ellena, 'I didn't know it was this easy to make Mum and Dad happy.

How lucky I am to have such great parents!'

...and she snuggled up to them,

...for the best hug ever!

The End

Safari Children's Books on Good Behavior

www.safarichildrensbooks.com

The Safari Children's Books
on Good Behavior